THE KING

ELIAS C. SAMPAIO

WESTBOW
PRESS®
A DIVISION OF THOMAS NELSON
& ZONDERVAN

WestBow Press books may be ordered through
booksellers or by contacting:

WestBow Press
A Division of Thomas Nelson & Zondervan
1663 Liberty Drive
Bloomington, IN 47403
www.westbowpress.com
844-714-3454

Scripture taken from the King James Version of the Bible.

ISBN: 978-1-6642-8876-8 (sc)
ISBN: 978-1-6642-8877-5 (e)

Library of Congress Control Number: 2023900336

Print information available on the last page.

WestBow Press rev. date: 03/10/2023

SI VIS
PACEM, PARA
BELLUM.
IF PEACE, PREPARE
FOR WAR.

CONTENTS

ACKNOWLEDGMENTS

I want to shine a light on the person who helped me write and publish my books! Anna Z Sampaio.

(Proverbs 18:22 KJV) "Whoso findeth a wife findeth a good thing, and obtaineth favour of the Lord."

Amen, a blessing I have gained from the Lord. To have found a diamond so rare and beautiful, my Lord has been good. The rarity of her beauty is overwhelming, and none can compare. A miner can dig all his life searching for her, yet he will not find her. The favor of a good wife is not quickly gained; to obtain it, one must explore the coldest of places, the darkest of caves, just for a glimpse of the shine of a yet unpolished diamond, waiting to be discovered by a brave miner seeking favor. The women of our lives are often pushed back by this wild life, as we tend to notice all crucial things only when it's too late! But now, I seek to polish this diamond of favor.

I have been so lucky to have stumbled into the unknown, the rarest of diamonds Anna Z Sampaio, my love! The woman who stands by my side! Thank you for supporting me on this journey!

CHAPTER  one

As I stand in this once peaceful and fruitful land, these eyes have witnessed my destruction. My enemies have successfully crippled my army to nothing; the will to fight has been drained out of their hearts as a snake wraps around its prey, squeezing until its last breath is taken. I would imagine this is what drowning in the lowest depth must feel like, an immense amount of pressure! How could my end be so shameful with no glorious act of value, strength, or even character! Oh, how I have failed my kingdom.

Those who have remained are now captive to my enemy's wrath. My path is now unclear. Mine and my soldiers' purpose are faint. Will there be a day of salvation for us? Will our allies come to our aid, or will they turn away from our defeat in shame? If only I had been more cautious in combat. Maybe if I had held my ambitions aside? My ego was too great. How the mighty have fallen, they will say.

I wonder if being so blind and foolish is common

in young rulers who have much to gain from this world! Youth is filled with life and energy to explore the unknown! So, it is only natural for the young to seek other kingdoms to conquer for their glorious growth. The young dream of tomorrow conquests when the long-forgotten seeks the pearls of wisdom of today. Oh, if I had only heard the voice of wisdom. If only I had taken the time to turn my ear towards her voice. If only I..., I.

"Where is the King?" a deep-toned shout from the Warlord himself. "Where is the mighty warrior who barked and barked at us from afar?" The Warlord's words travel over the surrounding battlefield like an eagle gliding in the air; were his words hovering over the fallen army.

The Warlord approaches the broken and shameful King, and He proceeds to humiliate the King in front of all who remain alive on the desolated battlefield. "Ah!" with a menacing smile, the Warlord says to the King. "I have found you, dog! Your speech is big, but your actions are small!"

As the King was defeated in battle by his enemy, his mind became lost in his failure. The Warlord's words could not reach the shattered King's ear. "What's the matter?" says the Warlord in a sarcastic tone. "Oh, mighty King, come on, give us a shout! Shout like the big bad lion you claimed to be."

The King falls to his knees before the Warlord

due to the shame of defeat. "What... what will..." with a miserable stutter, the King pushes for words to come out. "...what will happen...to...to my men?" the King asked.

Standing over the dishonorable King, the Warlord reaches out his hands towards the King's bowed head as he proceeds to forcefully lift the King's eyes towards the battlefield. "Your men?" replied the Warlord. "Take a good look around you." the Warlord continues to speak to the King. "Those you call your men now belong to the mud! This muddy graveyard will be your glorious legacy!" shouts the Warlord with a wicked laugh. "You know, it's hard to believe this was a lovely field just a few hours ago." says the Warlord, as they both look out into what remains. The King has lost everything.

Emotions are overwhelming me, and my vision is flooding with painful tears. My enemy stands before me; I see his mouth speaking through the waters of my eyes, but my ears do not hear a word. There is a low yet heavy pounding that seems to be blocking all surrounding noise as I try to speak an utter in the hopes that my enemy will spare my men. The mystery of this empowering thumping becomes revealed as my own heart! It's as if the pain is too great to bear in isolation, so in desperation, this lonely heart attempts to break free from the captivity of my chest. My hands grip against my heart so it may be still; I must remain calm.

The Warlord realizes the King's mind fell into despair. So out of despisement that the King wasn't listening to him speak, he advances to pound the King into the muddy ground. "You fool! Listen to me when I am speaking." the Warlord shouts towards the King as he leads rageful stomps onto the grounded King.

"What a foolish king you are!" he continued to shout louder. "You're so self-involved that you've probably overcome by selfish emotions." says the Warlord, becoming more enraged with every word as if it were unfair for the King to feel more pain from his thoughts than the punishment the Warlord has in mind for him.

"What a waste of possibility; I could have shown you the wonderful things still to come" With disappointment in his voice, the Warlord looks in the direction of the King's kingdom. "I guess it's too late; your end has come." He raises his sword and chops off the King's head. The head of the fallen King begins to slide away in the mud and is picked up by one of his men. "THE KING IS DEAD!" roars the Warlord.

In the darkness of night, you might hear the yell of someone woken up by fear. It is an inevitable fear surrounding the mind, with voices and visions of their demise. The fear of evil, the fear of failure, the fear of death: Nightmare is a name we give to discard our fearful vision as nothing more than a bad dream.

"Ah!" screams the King. "My head! I'm alive..." says the King as this vision shakes him. "Oh, thank the lord." begs the King. "It was only a nightmare," he tells himself in hopes of achieving peace of mind, but a small voice remains in the shadows of the King's mind. *Is my end so unclear? What must I do? In moments of hesitation, what must a King do? Is he truly meant to push forward, unaware of survival?* Unsure of his safety, or is he to flee away from his enemies, is to hide, revealing weakness?

How do we measure a king's rule, his strength? Is it by the size of his army, the prosperity of his kingdom, or maybe the greatness of his mind, the path he walks? This question few kings understand; most rule by might alone, and only few lead with wisdom and understanding over their people. Yet knowledge and understanding mean nothing when foreign armies overcome you. When your kingdom becomes consumed with fire, what will wisdom serve? Tell me! By what is a king's honor measured? By what is my strength measured?

When I fall to the ground defeated before my enemy, what will my KINGDOM be MEASURED? Tell me, for what will they remember me?

A voice calls out for the King from outside his tent, concerned with the King's wellness. "My lord, the day has arrived."

"Oh, has the hour of war come already?" replies the King, with an uncomfortable voice.

"What shall I instruct your army today?"

asked Legatus, the legion commander. But the King did not respond, for his attention was still on his vision. "My lord, have you decided on the course of our assault?" since the King ignored the first question, Legatus continued to push for a much-needed answer.

"What has the scout reported?" the King asked Legatus.

"Report says this self-proclaimed Warlord has 3,000 of his men camped out by the fields. And he is not far behind them, in a separate camp guarded by another 2,000 men. Compared to our legion of 6,000, we ought to have the upper hand, my lord!"

As Legatus informs the King of their tactical advance in warfare, the holy King becomes more doubtful of what is true. Dreams of death have clouded his sight. "Legatus, do you have faith in this victory?" the King asked with a great interest for a sincere response.

Legatus, with a surprised look, spoke with an encouraging voice. "My lord, faith is not needed! Your army's strength alone is unmatched in battle. All nations fall to fear before your great majesty!"

"Stop this nonsense!" shouts the King, cutting off Legatus's speech of confidence. With a deep-rooted concern for his men, the King reveals his dream, "I had a vision of death; I ask you now with the truth! What will our outcome be in this battle?"

"My Lord, forgive me. But I speak truthfully;

we have the numbers to support our claims to victory." replies Legatus. "Your dream, my lord, must have been a misinterpretation." expresses he to the King to lift the good King's aspirations.

"Leave me, I must think." orders the King.

"Yes, my lord!" are Legatus's final words with the King before he leaves the tent.

The fool, faith is unnecessary. Faith is everything in battle; one cannot win by numbers alone. The warmest heart from one rebel is mightier than ten heartless warriors; to believe in tomorrow is the most potent weapon any man can have. Ah, even I knowing faith is all that I need. Why are these visions holding me captive? I must calm myself; these nightmares of mine are not visions.

The King carrying a heavy burden within his heart, walks out of his tent, strolling across his holy army's campground, analyzing every battle formation he could put together. His highest commanding officers await his final order; the King's legion has been ready for war. They all have prepared themself for death; the men speak only of today; tomorrow will be known purely for the victorious.

CHAPTER  two

After hours of strategic planning in his mind, the King has finally found a path to victory in the campaign to overthrow the Warlord from his evil crusade. The faithful King joins the five commanding officers to position his plans into motion, the five who overlook 6,000 men.

"At this moment, from the report we received, we must attack two military camps. Holding a sum of 5,000 men." announces the King to his trusted commanding officers. "Tell me, Angusticavii, will our cavaliers be able to reach their guards in time to stop them from alerting the second camp?"

The fourth in command, Tribuni Angusticavii, leads the loyal knights. "Yes, my lord! Our knights should be able to outrun their stallions."

"Very good. Regarding our ground troops, will they be able to endure the long journey?"

Primus Pilus is fifth in command, as he leads the first file of foot soldiers. "My lord! My men are strong in faith and highly motivated. In your name, they will fight to the death! The journey may be difficult once our first battle commences, but they will succeed."

"Faith will be needed, for today will be a day many will speak on! I trust operations are in good faith?" asked the King.

"Yes, my lord! We have prepared the men to give our lives if needed! We fight for the kingdom." replies Praedectus Castrorum, the third in charge of the military operations.

"My lord, we have been awaiting your command!" says Tribunus Laticavius, second in command to the legion army here.

"I congratulate all of you; your work has not been in vain." announces the King. "For generations to come, the people of our kingdom will remember your names! Your memory will not fade away into time. We will wipe our enemies from history, and only we will remain!"

Now only outranked by the King, the legionary commander Lagutus Legionis. The right hand of his holiness questions the King. "My lord, what have you planned?"

"Lagutus, my friend, we shall attack the first camp with full force. Our numbers will be the advantage in the first battle, and we shall cut down their only lifeline to the Warlord. By splitting our forces in two, we will be able to surround them. Our primary attack will be a direct hit to the front gates;

before this, we will send out the second company with the more agile fighters flanking the first camp undetected, so when chaos rises at the gates, our men shall set a wall of fire and destruction at the back of their camp blocking all routes that lead towards the Warlord's second camp. When he notices the dark fumes of death engulfing his plans, he has no choice but to rush to save his people. The urgent ride they will make to protect their men from our hands. will drain their force, and we shall strike them at their most fragile moment. Death will find them as they run to save their own; we shall be awaiting their arrival. By the time the Warlord arrives, we will have conquered their first camp. Our arrows shall bring a warm welcome to this impulsive Warlord, and they will know who we are! The kingdom will not fall; they will not be ready. The kingdom will stand with truth and power." declares the King with a mighty voice.

"My lord, I believe you have found a path to victory." says Lagutus Legionis. Then all the four commanders together reply, "For the kingdom!"

"Now tell the men, we leave within the hour!" orders the King.

The five roar, "Yes, my lord!"

The five commanders prepare the men for a glorious battle against the Warlord's crusade. The soldiers' mood quickly changed from an uncomfortable sensation into an intense and infectious victorious spirit for war.

There is a small village not far from the good King's campsite. The very first who will witness a crusade by fire and destruction if the Warlord becomes the victor in tomorrow's crucial battle. The good people of this village are faithful to their beloved King, and they would never doubt his power to save them. But even in good faith, they could feel an unease spirit traveling through the passing winds from the King's campsite as current is ever-changing, as it flows through the lands of this earth, from hurricanes to peaceful breeze. The people of this beautiful village received a joyful gust of wind coming from the King's campsite; The triumphant songs seemed to belong to a festival rather than an army preparing for war. Hearing delightful chants from a legion of warriors heading into battle must be a pleasant relief for this lonely village.

Now finally, the full power of the holy army is set for war, only waiting for the royal command. All fully armored, from horses to archers, none shows any weakness in their stand. The King's attack is mighty as his shield, perfectly balanced from the sharpest blades to the deadliest arrowheads. His commanders lead with wisdom and courage, understanding defeat is not far from victory. At any given moment, the course of battle could change against them. To be of a calm mind, faithful in the most dreadful, the belief of tomorrow's sunrise is more vital than yesterday's darkest moonless night. The King approaches his men to give them a grandiose speech as if it was from heaven itself.

"The actions we take today will leave a mark in time... History will speak of today, no matter who remains. The flesh will shed its blood and return to its soil... I only ask you this: To what ends will your story go? To what ends?! What shall be your final chapters? Will your youthful soul die here and now, or will you live to be old and fat, to see the kingdom come? Our kingdom is in your hands, and its future is yours to control! The spark of your life is the true power of our mighty kingdom. You are the kingdom! The pen of destiny is in your hands now! So, write with glorious words your final chapter. For in your hands lays the foundation for glory! You will write your end, no one else; you have the power! So, I ask you, men of domains and fortune, what ends will you go? What shall the pages of our life utter?!" shouts the King towards his legion.

The roar of 6,000 men greeted the King's words. "For the kingdom, we fight! For the realm, we live! To end, we march! To end, we march! All hail the King!" roars the holy army.

With a warm and joyful noise, the King commands his army to move to battle. "Then let us go and create a glorious story!" The holy army marches towards the fields to pursue the Warlord's campsite, with their plans entirely in motion. Their souls march vigorously like lions on the hunt, the very ground trembles before them.

CHAPTER  three

Six thousand men march towards war, 6,000 men marching with one goal; a massive military strength marches within these fields. The very ground trembles as the boots of each man press on towards writing a new chapter! The melodies of the men roam around the winds giving them an unnatural atmosphere. Tall and far between trees, furry yet small bushes and blooming yellow flowers seem to dance alongside the passing winds rejoicing in the coming of the holy army. A magnificent view stood before the King, his men roaring as lions marched into the blossoming victory awaiting the other side of the field. A picture too powerful for words, emotions too strong to recite, when even mother nature reveals her hand, a site to see for any conquering king.

"Castrorum, what have you heard exactly about this warlord?" Angusticavii asks as he rides alongside. But Praedectus Castrorum, the third in charge of the military operations, remained silent. "Castrorum, I am talking to you." Angusticavii whispers again.

"Fool, I don't know any more than you do about that man!" Castrorum shouts, taking the attention of Tribunus Laticavius, second in command to the legion army.

"Commanders, are you fighting again? You two can't get along, huh?" Laticavius comments as he introduces himself into the conversation.

"Angusticavii, what have you done now?" asks Laticavius, suggesting Castrorum has grown tired of all the games they play.

"Forgive me, my lord; I wondered if Castrorum knows anything of this Warlord." Angusticavii answers.

"I've only heard rumors, nothing to be true. The men told me that he has already destroyed his own country in search of glory, and now he seeks to do the same here in our lands. The Warlord is a demon, not a man, as all rumors go. Years ago, he lost his soul; he gave it up for unheard power. That his soldiers are only after blood, and death itself holds the joy of their hearts. But all are rumors. Just another wild man, creating false names, false realities, all to fulfill a wild fantasy. But today, that dream ends, my lord." Laticavius offers only a glance towards Angusticavii to say these rumors he speaks of are far from the truth. "A wild fantasy would be nice." Laticavius murmurs to himself as he rode ahead of the two commanders.

"What's his problem?" Angusticavii continues to speak, but no one will hear him; Angusticavii loses his voice to the world around him.

Six thousand men marched to defeat an evil not fully known, not fully understood. The truths they hold are few, but truths they are! The truth of pain and suffering fact that when death comes knocking, you do not wait; you do not greet it with warmth and kindness. Instead, you welcome it with passion and fire! The force of love, joy, and spirit! The fire of life, dreams, and youth! The kingdom knows this to be the truth – people who stand by with courage and good faith. Hence the reason, the holy army has a magical atmosphere surrounding them.

Up in front of the legion, two scouts ride 10 miles ahead to ensure the safety of the trail.

As they approached the enemy's first camp, their orders were to hold a secure position, gain access to the base, and send word back by pigeon. in the letter; the message was to inform the King of three specific concerns. The first, locate the identity of the Warlord. The second, discover all critical strongholds' vulnerability. The third, deliver the information at all costs. Without this crucial knowledge of the enemy's strength, it could mean the end of their kingdom. The two scouts understood their role in the war; those who see the next move in battle will always pave the road to victory.

CHAPTER  four

The two reached the enemy's camp by nightfall, and they hid their horses two miles away from the campsite. They knew the only way to pass the guards undetected would be by foot, from crawling under desolate trees to climbing wretched hills.

The two rushed through the darkness as they traveled light, each with a tiny dagger hanging from the left side of their waist, a perfect weapon designed for up-close and intimate attacks. Also, each man brought a small bird tied up into a miniature cage, dangling from their right side. Its only purpose is to deliver the intel as swiftly as possible. And finally, a bow fastened to their backs combined with two arrows – the weapon of inevitable invasion from the unknown.

Now, the camp is in the open area of fields; the Warlord's men are rumored to be highly skilled warriors, never vulnerable to a surprise attack.

"Ammiel, I heard a story; their men fall from the sky like flying demons?" the scout Shaphat whispers with a troubled tone in his voice.

"Relax, if demons are they, we will be like the sun!" replies Ammiel.

"The sun... what does that mean?" Shaphat says with a confused look towards Ammiel.

"The sun is bright, and demons are dark. We will make them blind with our zeal." Ammiel answers with a laugh. But Shaphat shows zero humor. The rumors he heard feel too real as they journey through the darkness of the night. by this time, they can see the border of the camp. "Shaphat, keep your eyes open." Ammiel whispers.

"Got it." Shaphat responds.

Each step forward now is met with unworldly pressure. The camp's firepit location is in the center, but its warmth and intensity seem to overflow throughout the open field and the surrounding forest.

Shaphat taps Ammiel on the shoulder, directing him to a high point at the edge of the woods overlooking the camp.

The two scouts reach the high end with caution and dreadfulness, worrying about what terrors they might discover to be true.

"Well, Shaphat, I don't see any monsters, do you?" Ammiel mocks, for all they find are ordinary men. The enemy's camp is pleasing; there linger no monsters. Their eyes are witnessing nothing more than simple men, men we see passing through the voyages of this life. Men whose identity is never known to us are the most uncomplicated of men, who are often vanished by the tremendous waves of the sea of life.

Shaphat begins to take notes of their camp's fortifications, every detail, and any possible threats that may hinder their attack.

"Have you noticed; their watchman is not here?" Ammiel mentions as he looks around with concern. "Shaphat... Do you see any of them?" Ammiel whispers as he turns towards his partner in awe of his silence, but his eyes greet him with horror.

A blade ran across Shaphat's neck, shattering his spinal cord and triggering Shaphat's body to become stiff.

Ammiel quickly acts, snatching the note out of his partner's hands as they tightly grip the last words he has written. Ammiel begins running to escape from an invisible opponent; the thoughts of how, when, and from where the attack could have come instantly pass through his mind. Ammiel begins to roll up his partner's last words to send ahead of him with the pigeon. But doubts choke his mind, for his salvation is still two miles away. Would he be able to make it out alive?

Unfortunately, Ammiel's vision becomes blurry in the darkness as he runs away, looking around, attempting to intercept the next murderous attack. Ammiel trips on a root of a tree. He rolls on his back, facing the heavens; maybe it was just a man. But the final glimpse Ammiel, the scout to the Holy army, sees is an unearthly figure leaping from the treetops, piercing his heart with the coldest tip of death's blade. Even the most foolish of rumors can become truth in moments of despair.

CHAPTER  five

Now on the third day, the King and his legion have arrived at the borders of the fields. Only five miles away from the Warlord's first campsite, the Holy army determinedly awaiting the final report before they dispatch to all-out war.

"My liege... my King!" a voice shouts from the back ranks of the legion army, capturing the attention of all. "My King, we have received it! The two, they did it! They have successfully infiltrated the enemy's camp; we have the letter with its full description. they are looking forward to our attack." The voice continues to shout until he reaches the Holy King. The voice belongs to a small youth whose aid to the legion is nothing more than a helping hand to transport the equipment. However, his voice casts out a heavy calling of courage and faith.

"Give it to me, boy!" orders Lagutus Legionis.

"Well, my friend,what does it say?" asks the King.

"My lord, all we hoped for is true. We can continue with our plans. This report confirms they will fall to our assault. Their guards don't expect any coming invasion; they are indeed few; our strategy of attacking with two companies will work. The second company will travel light and move to the positions they have marked for us. We will overtake them without a struggle. They will fall by noon; the scouts have done well, my lord." replies Lagutus.

"What of the Warlord? Is there any word of my request?" asks the King with concern.

"No mention of the Warlord, my King. But I assure you today is his last." Lagutus boldly proclaims.

"I understand... commanders prepare to move! Today, tell your men, triumph awaits them!" the King orders the legion towards invasion!

The Holy King and his commanders position themselves in the center of the legion army to provide a strong influence during battle. The four leading war generals are arranged: from Angusticavii on the far left, leading with his knights, to Castrorum holding the center-left of his Holy King's army. Now, from the far-right, Laticavius, second in charge of the legion, rides with the men suited for their extraordinary mission as Lagutus Legionis leads the center-right, the faithful and first commander of the company.

Finally overseeing all stands the King in the center of everything, just like a multitude of planets revolves around the sun's gravitational pull, as the King's gravity in battle.

Every soldier fighting carries within them the potential exploration and advancement of new worlds, and they all come together with the purpose to live for a greater kingdom.

What gain is there in outer world explorations when the minds and souls of our fellow man hold an infinite possibility for a better tomorrow?

Towards tomorrow's sunrise, the legion marches onward.

CHAPTER

SIX

They reach the two-mile mark where Laticaviusw and his men must depart from the company and rush ahead to pull off the rear attack in time.

"Straight path to victory lays the road ahead! Laticavius, do not lose faith in our creed or the legion. We will meet at the end of the day to celebrate our glory!" shouts the King to Laticavius as he leads his men in the direction of the marked locations the scouts informed them to meet and prepare the flank assault.

The legion has split up into two separate campaigns, the main attack line holding 5,000 men and knights, the other of 1,000 men highly skilled hand-to-hand combats warriors leading the charge for the lifeline of their second camp. Both attacks will happen simultaneously.

"We must hurry! Our brothers are expecting us to bring the camp to ashes. Our King will keep them busy in the front of the camp while we bring fire and death from behind, so hurry up; time is against us!" Laticavius orders the men with a roar to run.

The men running through the forest following the path marked in the letter for them, 1,000 men rushing through the wood's trees and bushes, leaving a trail of ruin behind. Since time is against them, they are not concerned with stealth anymore, for they know the King will take all their attention away from them. The King's army will march straight ahead, announcing their claim to victory. If any guard is to see the rear attack coming, it will not matter; the King will be knocking at the camp's front doors with his crusade for justice.

"Commander, looks like we are approaching the location marked on the letter." says a soldier as he reads the notes marking a specific location for them to go through before arriving at the camp's rear. "Just over this hill, and we should see Ammiel and Shaphat again," the soldier says as they take the final steps.

In men's hearts, hope and desires are found, fueled by the eyes that see far beyond what our hands can reach and grab. The dreams and hope for a better tomorrow are just beyond the horizon. This hope is evident in the heart of the men running over this very hill, their eyes filled with hope and ambition to bring justice to the Warlord's evil crusade.

The view over the mountain does not always bring joy. The soldiers encounter the sight of two dead bodies hanging upside down, tied up in separating branches from the big tree in the middle of the open square in the forest. The rope ran ten feet down until the knot tied to their ankles.

"Hold soldiers, we are not alone!" shouts Laticavius when he lays eyes on the bodies realizing the two corpses are Ammiel and Shaphat.

All the men stop and form two lines standing back-to-back, each trusting the other to provide cover, leaving Laticavius in front to lead.

"I don't understand... weren't they successful." whispers a soldier standing near the front line.

"It's a trap! Quickly send word to the King before it's too late!" Laticavius orders to send the word to the end of the line. Immediately the last soldier takes off running to warn the King of the enemy's trap.

Unfortunately, it is too late. The men begin to fall as arrows rain down on them from the tops of the trees. In one moment, 999 men fell before the Warlord. Laticavius and his men died.

"It's a trap! It's a trap! They know we're coming!" screams the soldier as he runs back through the path they came. "My king..." is the final words expressed out of this faithful soldier's lungs before two arrows penetrate through him, leaving him to fall bleeding to death on the path that was meant to bring liberation.

Back in the main legion force, the King is on a direct course towards the camp, unaware of any new updates on Laticavius and his men. The Holy Army is now more than ever at their most anticipated moment, the calm before the storm. Only a few yards away, the Warlord's campsite is now visible.

"There it is, my King, just as the spies wrote, two watchtowers armed with polyabolos arrow shooter if we wish to have no casualties on our end. We must stay out of range until our men on the other side can drive them out with the flames. My lord, we must make them bring the fight to us," Lagutus informs the King.

"Yes, very well then." responds the King. "Sound the signal for war. Let them know that we are here!" orders the King.

The Holy Army roars their war chants with golden trumpets, and a sound wave of the roar thrusts itself towards the Warlord's camp, turning every flag, banner, and slack of every loosened tent garment to collide against the wind. Minutes pass, and no response comes from the camp; the roaring of the Holy Army ends with a stillness from the enemy, and not a single life appears before them.

"Something is wrong." Lagutus mumbles.

Then after what seems to be hours of silence, a lone man riding his horse strolls out from the camp's front gate. No fear, without caution, just a simple stroll, as if he was taking in the view of a beautiful day in the forest instead of walking into a battlefield. Not once does he look upon the legion and turns his head back, looking for help; this man armored in black steel stands in between the King's Holy Army and the Warlord's camp alone.

"Oh, mighty King... how far have you come..." speaks the man with a low yet demanding tone, a tone ears tend to lean towards attempting to grab hold of those last few words at the end of whispers, whispers that tend to float in the air longer so it can hope to land on open ears.

"Where is your leader?! Where is your army?! Do you come to us for surrender?!" Lagutus shouts at the lone man interrupting him.

"Surrender?" mumbles the man as he turns his eyes towards the legion's soldiers. "Surrender... what value... does a man have if he surrenders to his enemy?" the man responds.

"Just who are you to stand so bold before my army?" questions the King.

"I am he, who you know so little about, he who you strive to destroy," the man answers, reviling himself to be the Warlord.

The King reaches for his sword and commands the legion to kill him at this exact moment; Chaos breaks out, the King lifts his sword in the air, and a storm of arrows begins to rain down from the surrounding forest. Soldiers in the outer flanks dropped dead, and the King and the men in the inner center pushed forward, aiming for only one target, the Warlord. But after the arrows, the Warlord's men come running into the battle, and a chaotic struggle begins between them. The strategic battle is long gone. The Warlord is successful in turning the tides of war in his favor.

The legion might have been more extensive and more equipped for long periods of battle, but now they are cornered into a brawl. Skill is not a factor anymore; packed together, leaving no room to swing a sword at will, the Warlord's men rush and bash the legion into fists and throws, body slams that lead to a cluster of armors jammed together.

Heaven and earth meet in moments of conflict, and souls of cursed men travel across history, witnessing their creation and annihilation. The hands of men carry generations and generations of madness. The legion army is no different from this cursed fate; good men will fall, blood will spill, and when the heavens and earth reunite in wartime. No sound or evil man will stray away from the horrors of war. Dust of men is joined in the flow of time by blood on the grounds of battle, where creation and destruction meet.

CHAPTER  seven

Desperation fills the atmosphere with despair — one full hour of horrifying sound and events unfolding in this land. Many dead have become unrecognizable, and many living has become unredeemable to the meadows in life. Still, a fight to live on must happen when once it was a fight to bring joy and deliverance to a broken-spirited people. It is now desperation for survival.

The Warlord and the King face each other in battle. "Oh, thy king, what fancy sword you wield." the Warlord says, mocking the King.

"Shut up, you monster! I will kill you for what you have done!" rages the King.

The two men take a moment to look upon the desolated warzone; one feels grief and regret, while the other smiles and laughs...

"What value does a man have in surrender?" the Warlord murmurs as he looks towards heaven.

"None... this... this is why you fight to the bitter

end?" says the King greeting his enemy into a final fight.

The two armies have been beaten, dragged, and suffocated on the muddy ground, so it is hard to tell who is genuinely winning. Most of the remaining soldiers have stopped fighting, holding on to their last breath as they look for the King's duel to be the deciding factor in this battle. The King thrusts his sword forward as the Warlord looks up at the sky but instantly, the Warlord reacts; they clash swords. A series of wild sword swings come from the King as he gives all his strength to take down his enemy. Back and forth, they go swing after swing; at times, one misses, and at other times one lands a punch or a push, a dual just as ugly and dirty as the one which started it all.

Then after some time, the two swords clash once more, but they do not retract; instead, the men push forward, opposing each other's power on the other; only the strongest will prevail. "For the kingdom!" roars the King as his sword begins to scrape the Warlord's helmet. The King's victory is in sight just a little more, and the head of evil will be severed. During the dual, the battlefield has become silent; everyone's eye is focused on what will be the outcome; in the Warlord's final moments, the sound of metal scraping on metal is interrupted by a maniacal laugher by the Warlord himself.

"You yell *'for the kingdom!'* I will burn your beloved kingdom to ashes." says the Warlord mocking the words of the King. "Do you know who I am?" the Warlord questions the Holy King.

"You are evil!" responds the King.

"Wrong!" shouts the Warlord as he lunges towards the King's legs, breaking their balance as they fall to the ground. The Warlord jumps on top of the King and wraps his hands around the neck. The King, with his back to the ground doing everything in his power to escape, his enemy commences whispering into his ear. "I am the voice... the voice that creeps up in the back of your mind... the whisper of despair that you can't escape... you are powerless against me... because I am the poison in your body...the blur in your vision... you can never destroy me; I live inside you, I know all your weakness, I am the reaper of death." whispers the Warlord into Holy King's ears as he takes his final gasp for air. The end of the legion army and all their beloved kingdom.

The end.

CHAPTER  eight

"si vis pacem, para bellum."

Thank you! Thank you! And thank you!

I am not an author, so the fact that you read this little story of mine. It truly means a lot to me; this story isn't perfect. It has its flaws, but in a world where movies with zero writing talent/ effort make billions of dollars every year, I hope you enjoy it enough to tell your friends to pick up a copy to read today! That so, I may make billions of dollars of bad writing. (That is a joke.)

This story of the King and his Holy Army is loosely based on (Acts 19:13-20 KJV) when the sons of Jewish leaders, alongside a group of men, attempted to cast out a demon using Jesus's name, but we all know it didn't end so well for them.

Now I didn't write this book with the idea of just retelling (Acts 19:13-20 KJV) in a different light. But it was for a deeper meaning. The storytelling was just me attempting to be more of an author, but I need more time to grow. Time is an opportunity for the young.

When I wrote my first book *"Entangled: The soldier who dares to achieve miracles."* I had just finished school at CFNI. I never wanted to write or be an author in my life. *"Entangled"* was me listing to a piece of advice my teacher told us in class.

"Write your sermons as if you're telling a story so that it won't just point A, B, C. people remember stories better than clip notes."

I don't remember what he said word by word, but you get the point.

So, I did, and it got to where I told myself to turn it into a book. It was long enough for it. I never thought of myself as an author, but things happen, and here we are now on my second book and a third book idea on the way! It's been about a year since I wrote *"Entangled,"* and lots has happened in life since then. My fiancée turned into my wife; I was anointed as a pastor and put in leadership over the youth at my church, "Igreja Tabuas Da Lei – Stones of Law Church." One can say I got thrown into several heavily responsible positions at once. Only the strongest survive, and there is only one way to get robust, and it's by moving heavyweight until it becomes lightweight.

All that to say. Lately, I have been thinking more about what everything means in our Christian church world and what the next generation has to fight.

A quick background of how I grew up: I could never fit in the real world or the church world. I mean the fake, pride hungry, sexually broken world when I say the real world, where you see people for the worst they can be. I could never fit in the church world, where everyone is a saint, the holy of holy in this world, the best humanity offers. Now I could never fit in because I saw both worlds as one.

Now I know you must be confused or curious about what type of church background I grew up in, but I can explain it in my third book!

But seriously, there is a version of the real vs. fake world in everyone's mind regarding the church. What I mentioned is just something minor, but maybe someone might have thought about it in their lives.

My point is – I didn't grow up with youth services every Friday night; I was the only youth in my family's church that went to church. When I was about eighteen or twenty, the church started to have actual youth services. I can't say I had grown up with it by then, but I have been a part of it in my early adult life.

What leads to the reason for writing this book. I am now a youth pastor, and we have been talking, discussing, and understanding our roles and the importance of the youth's rise into church leadership for the better of tomorrow. Today's youth will be tomorrow's pastors and leaders. But if they receive horrible teachings and horrific examples of what it means to be a leader today, then tomorrow is doomed.

This book speaks to those who desire to lead an army for God and bring genuine change into this world.

If we Christians believe the church is in a spiritual battle with the wicked world, why do we lack wisdom and understanding?

We battle more with each other than the devil in our own country. Nowadays, we only judge and criticize other Christians, never give the time to listen and understand where they are coming from. We are quick to yell and shut the doors we don't like. The people have designed the most popular Christian YouTube channels to spread gossip and divisions among Christians. Spreading shame, lies, and false teachings. We bring shame to the Holy Spirit by uplifting and chanting free Barabbas as we dress and walk like the Pharisees.

Let's stop this disgraceful rollercoaster of betrayals in the church from members, leaders, and pastors.

No one is free of guilt; we all have a part to play. Now understand what I am saying here: I do not condone defending the actions of the offense, one my read and miss appreciate my point. The church as a whole is fighting a losing battle.

I am not an author; I am not a genius; I am nobody. I am just a man attempting to bring a revolution to save tomorrow. This book will take a deeper look at the meaning of the church world, the unity of church members, and their role on the battlefield.

CHAPTER nine

"The vision is always inward spiritual growth, transform leaders, not followers, inspired by Godly unity." Something I wrote at the beginning of my time leading the youth.

The great apostle Paul writes to the church of Corinthians, explaining and teaching many things for them to learn. He showed the correct approach to the church world (the Christian lifestyle of their time). When the Holy Spirit movement was more endorsed than condemned, the people were coming to the church for a real change. The church was seeking the extraordinary activity of the Holy Spirit; they were not ashamed of it, but they urged it.

The ordinary people of his time had multiple religions, cultures, and oppressors to influence their mob mentality.

Now I'm not a historian, I might be wrong in this statement, but I can't see the promise of a heavenly kingdom awaiting them after death, serving only to express that the hardships of this life will be worth it in the end. I don't think that to be a strong enough reason for them to believe in Jesus.

Nothing is new under the sun. We can see that the hope for heaven has become less critical in the common mind of today's world. We the people see today, and we want to be pharos today! We are willing to die with all our belongings today! Tomorrow is someone else's problem; our only desire is to see paradise now. "Live your best life now; seek all your fleshly desires today!"

Nothing is new under the sun. So the church started to grow back in the day with this idea and understanding of the Holy Spirit and heaven. They had no name, no history, and lots of different opportunities from the popular culture, religion, and laws promising a better life after death.

Why would the church grow so much, only expressing "If you only believe in Jesus and no one else, then you will truly be saved at the end."

Why would the people suffer persecution only on a command religious theology of heaven?

What I think to be the correct answer is the Holy Spirit! The promise in (Acts 1:8 KJV) "The Helper!" Word of a supernatural Godly movement that changed everything you believed as truth is now false would spread like wildfire!

What the pagan religions attempted to imitate but never could, a power you didn't have to kill or drink some animal's blood, a force received only by those who believe and walk out in the light of God. The power of Jesus's name is something worth finding out if it is real or not.

The Holy Spirit is the reason I believe the church grew; how else would pagan sorcerers repent in the name of Jesus. The ordinary person needs a supernatural intervention to receive real change.

The Holy Spirit is alive! We must not be ashamed of Him!

Unfortunately, our generation has lost its way. The movement of the Holy Spirit has become less and less authentic in modern-day Christianity.

The church is now a business, a concert, with star pastors and worship leaders who lead the crowds into wild dreams of triumph storytelling. It's turned into a joke; we praise the fake and shame the true. The commoner nowadays is so filled with artificial Glory that we as a whole believe it to be the Glory of God.

(John 8:7 KJV) "... He that is without sin among you, let him first cast a stone at her." And I'm not trying to judge which church is holy or not.

The argument with this book is not to bring more debates; the topic discussed concerns all churches of all people, and none is without fault.

The church is in a broken world; we, the people,

are as stubborn as a rock. We are unwilling to hear our brothers and sisters in the faith.

To prove my point, whatever your background is with the church, or religion, if I have written anything you disagreed with, then there is nothing I can say that would change your mind. Unless the Holy Spirit comes to you and reveals something new in a way that you may see my point or He reveals to me what I am not understanding.

Now I'm not saying I know it all, nor that I am speaking God's words to tell the world. Nope, not at all. I am nobody. You've never heard of me; I don't have a massive following. I am but a voice in the desert. I am just a man attempting to bring a revolution to save tomorrow.

So, as you read, keep this in mind: I am applying Paul's message of unity for the church to the art of war.

This book will break down every important character within the church and compare them to their chess embodiment.

Why chess? Chess is a strategic game where you lead an army into war – a war in which each soldier must do their part to win. It's a dark and dirty war until your king or your enemy's king has been suffocated to his death. Yes, the type of death that brings agony to all bystanders is a little dramatic. But this is chess, and it's a fair and balanced war. To be victorious, one must strive to find unity within his army, to lead without weakness. One careless move, one delayed attack, will cause your kingdom to fall.

So, my brother and sister, the Christian church is in a losing war, and the most potent weapon at our disposal has been lost to us for generations.

Please continue to read so you may find the unity we lack, the unity that has been replaced with notoriety. The church needs to learn to fight properly! For this reason, I am writing, so the next generation can learn to value the truth.

Si vis pacem, para bellum. If peace, prepare for war.

CHAPTER  ten

A gift in diversity, unity in one body.

Paul writes to the Corinthians in chapter 12 with the topic of diversity in mind. Paul explains to a group of complex human beings that God works in the middle of diversity with unity. Paul says that ministry lives in a multitude of gifts given only by the Lord, who works all in all.

Because (1 Corinthians 12:3 KJV) "... no man can say that Jesus is the Lord, but by the Holy Ghost."

Expressing to the Corinthians that their diversity is a good thing; we are not all meant to be exactly alike. Machines of machines thinking, moving, and living in perfect harmonization. It is a straightforward concept to understand, yet it is challenging to practice the way it was intended.

It is far easier to take this idea of diversity and God's work within it and abuse it with no end. This concept leads us towards the first step to understanding the chess game for God's kingdom and our critical part in this war.

Let's break down this first concept: the gift of diversity.

Now let me ask you this: How many different types of churches/ministries exist in your hometown? The answer is probably a lot. Out of all those obsessed God-loving people, how many truly walk out in the truth vs. those who twist it? The answer – nobody knows, only God.

But if I ask you, how many people or times has this concept of diversity twisted within your own home? *God will use/want me to be just the way I am! Who cares about character growth and maturing in God's world? Nope, God works with diversity; we are all not meant to be the same, I will be me, and you be you!*

Get where I'm going with the idea? Nowadays, there are gay churches, probably even alien-believing churches, etc. It's effortless to twist God's word to mean something he didn't intend for in our lives.

That is why the Holy Spirit is heavily essential for us to receive, to keep us from falling into hypocrisy and the profanity of His word.

How did it get to this? I could easily blame any older generation for not keeping God's words pure and just, but the church and its people have lost this battle for far too long. Right now is the only time we have to fix this, before it's too late.

Great is the need to properly understand/apply the diversity in the churches and its ministry within its people.

Paul writes not to encourage wild flesh behaviors but to stop the need to compare, compete, and imitate others within the ministry.

So, you can focus on your spiritual growth; you decide to live or die for Jesus. You control if your actions will be originally given by God or counterfeit to look like someone else's gift. Don't go around looking to recreate someone's ministry but seek God in your unique way. But hold on a minute! Don't follow your flesh! Grow in character and God's word, obey your leaders, and don't compare or imitate others; seek the authenticity of the Holy Spirit.

The first part of the gift of diversity follows the individual human function in God's kingdom to seek inward growth rather than fabricate an artificial outer skin.

The second part involves the collaboration involving the community of churches and its family trees. The roots of historic trees are rotting away in the ground by the lack of care and nurture from each passing generation, seeking to further push society into the future by leaving the past behind. Of course, these dying roots I speak about are the core belief of the church.

The church was created to tell the world that Jesus is the only way to cross from this world into a paradise kingdom, and we are here as His servants providing for the injured and sick. The church is to be a hospital for your mind and soul. Unfortunately, just like a hospital, corruption and greed can take over, leading the core reason for its inception to be a forgotten memory.

The new church leaders' intentions are more focused on explorations into franchises of their ministry (Starbucks coffee) instead of the quests into the supernatural ways of the Lord.

My point is that church organizations need to stop seeing other churches as potential franchise business partnerships, enemies, or rival competition. Always in war with each other, judging and criticizing the others' worship, word, or status, and treating others as less important or ineffective for any reason involving membership or income value.

Where is the *unity*? The unity to help without ego. Unity to build Glory to the Lord, not for the organizations' arrogance. But for *unity* to walk the second mile, what would the church world look like united in the correct application of diversity for the kingdom of God? I think it would look like heaven because that's the only place I see all churches of God finding Unity. The sad reality is that humanity is broken, and not everyone leads with God's desire. This dream of unity in diversity can only go so far here on earth until Jesus comes to bring it to its fulfillment in heaven.

Yet to all church leaders/members, this unity applies in your own body of the congregation, showing the proper way to lead individuals with unique gifts from God, to properly promote and demote members for the request of character growth.

Paul's message is one of inspiration. Do not be afraid to freely allow the expression of gifts from the Holy Spirit in your church. We must not abuse God's word and twist it into something evil. Be the solution, not the problem.

This book will focus on the core members of the church and their role in a war game called *chess*, the correct application for unity within diversity.

(1 Corinthians 12:1-11 KJV) speak on unique spiritual gifts for each individual; Paul expresses the idea that not all gifts are for everyone. From wisdom to knowledge, from faith to healing, they all serve a different intention within a person to preach the Gospel. Go! Preach the Gospel, and God will provide, for a worker is worthy of his food. (Matthew 10:5-15 KJV) "....go, preach, saying, The kingdom of heaven is at hand.

... for the workman is worthy of his meat."

In our Friday night youth service, we broke down each gift and examined the core concepts for their existence. We discussed possible reasons why Paul decided to write:

Gift of healing to one and another the working of miracles.

We worked on the idea and understanding that one's miracle prayer for healing might not be one's healing miracle prayer.

I hope that made sense to you as you read this because I'm not going to go that in-depth on each gift and its particular functions to improve a result to one's desire. If I did, I would never finish this book. I also doubt many people will read this far into it.

But anyways, breaking down each gift helps us understand a little more about unity within a diversity of gifts. The concept of teamwork is funded when you see each gift supports another, and none is more significant than another. Expect love, but we are not on the topic of love.

So, understanding diversity is good when applied within the boundary of people who do not compete, compare, or immediate others. Therefore, look towards growing inward spiritually so the God-given unique spiritual gifts can be revealed to us in the church to give proper Glory to the Most High!

CHAPTER  eleven

Now just who do you think you are?

The king or the queen? Not regarding the story I wrote in the beginning but to the chessboard. Are you a bishop or a rook? Maybe a pawn; who are you? What is your purpose for being part of the church?

Paul continues to develop in chapter 12, from verses 12 – 30, the idea of one body. The body has many functions, but they are all under one mind; the same goes for the body of Christ.

In the previous chapter, we talked a bit about diversity within church organizations. Well, in 12-30 verses, Paul wrote the prominent theme people receive is that every congregation of churches fits somewhere in the body of Christ, and that's where it usually ends with the idea that even if we are not all physically connected, we still all service Jesus Christ – justifying why we don't all have to agree on some specific details.

Such as how tall Jesus was, and if you have the correct height, you are holy, and the rest are all wicked. Get my point!

We usually see this section of Paul's writing to the Corinthians only for understanding each other's differences so that we may unite in Christ.

But we, on the other hand, will take this concept of one body with many parts and break it down into one church, not multiple churches under God. There is only one church to represent in chess, and the chess pieces will represent each fraction of that one church. Here is when you find out who you are! What your purpose is! And how to become an effective soldier for God's kingdom.

One empire contains one king, one queen, two bishops, two knights, two rooks, and eight pawns in chess. That is your army. The game's goal is to capture and kill your opponent's king, using every unique gift accessible to you by your soldiers. From the first moment you begin to play, every move you make will fall into one of three categories I like to call *attack*, *support*, or *move past*. There is a fourth, but we don't talk about it because only the fragile will withdraw from an enemy's threat. The player best prepared with strategic decisions throughout the game usually wins.

These categories I named are helpful to learn if you want to go out and evangelize. I talked with the youth about them and how we can approach people in tough conversations using this tactic, which I learned by playing chess.

Unfortunately, it doesn't do us any good here. What is good for us to understand here is how each piece moves along the board and what are their ties to the church.

But if you wish to know a little of my points of view on evangelism, how I think people can do better than hunting people around the parking lot forcing prayers and *Jesus loves you* down the throat until we repent and say I believe in Christ, leave a good review on amazon telling people to buy this book. Then maybe my fourth book will be about evangelism.

Let's get the ball rolling with who we are and what we are meant to do as the army of God's church. Paul writes that the head of the body is Christ, so the king of our military is Christ. Jesus Christ is the only Most High. If you thought or believed that you're important because you're somebody with a mini title in your name, forget about it! The only one we need to take order from is God, and He is the leader. That's the first important thing to know about the king in chess; He is our God.

The second is that we must do everything to protect Him from our enemy as his soldiers. That's our duty, and He believes in us to do so. Jesus said: what I have done, you will do greater things. The issue is that the modern church doesn't understand its role yet.

What is a king without his army? Dead, that's what he is!

The king doesn't move much in the game, and he is the frailest piece. Your whole army stops attacking every time your king is in danger. The focus is turned immediately to his defense, isn't that something. Imagine if something is threatening our God's dignity, reputation, or power; everyone in the body stops and focuses on solving the issue instead of leaving the church to die. What wonders would it bring?

I hope you can interpret what I'm saying in your own life, your church, your family, but most importantly, the reflection of God that you show the world. Because I will tell you, in the End Game of Chess, the king depends on the rooks and pawns to defend His Glory. A point I will make more explicit in the following few chapters as we discuss the roles of each soldier in more detail.

Right now, let's finish the position of the king, who represents our Lord. His wisdom and leadership should be seen and felt throughout the battlefield; even though he is the weakest, he is the essential part. Win or lose depends on the state of the king.

Some beginner chess players might feel like losing a queen is the same as losing the game if the opponent's queen is still active; that only happens when your confidence in your ability to fight is only supported by the notions of titles or hierarchy in your life. I know it can be a little confusing; the point I'm trying to make is when you place leaders or titles above God's will, you tend to fall into your enemy's hand like a puppet. You rise these entitled people so high they become gods among men, so when they fall as they will, you go down into despair, doubting life itself. That only happens when we forget that the king is only God's position and no one else is to be higher. That's all I have to say about the king in chess!

Before I go move on to the following pieces and what they mean, let me address why I am using this concept of chess, I am rated currently between 1200-1000 in ten minutes blitz, 1050-900 in three minutes blitz, and 1700-1600 in puzzles on chess.com. So, if you know anything, these numbers show I am just an average player. I understand just enough to make a remarkable book about it involving the church. That's just for me to say the metaphors I'm using can apply to our church world. The interaction within the game you experience can help you learn how to deal with problems and people in the real world. I'm not saying chess is anything spiritual, and it's not. The Bible and the Holy Spirit are All anyone will ever need to grow mentally and spiritually, but chess is an excellent game to help you become a better strategic person for solving problems with minor casualties.

Okay, let's finish the topic of the king. Don't let your King, our God look like a fool because of your lack of compassion, motivation, or understanding within the war to peace.

CHAPTER  twelve

Now I will ask again, just who do you think you are? What is your rank within the church? Are you a leader? Do you believe yourself to be someone of great importance? That if you disappeared today, nothing would get done right without you! The whole congregation will fall because you are not there to lead these pathetic people into the Glory of the Almighty!

The entitled leader is a fraud. The entitled identity that the church world has come to know is a disease to the people of God. We will focus on the attitude/mentality of these individuals with tiny labels beside their names.

I have an issue with the blunders/mistakes of those who come into power and choose to remain infected by this illness. Yes, I understand the church has a hierarchy system that everyone worldwide follows. And I do believe it is essential, but only when it is applied correctly with a

ELIAS C. SAMPAIO

leader who has true character, understanding, and humility. No matter what type of church organization you believe to be most holy. There is a structure designed for individuals to take charge and lead the congregation into battle. Leaders to help guide us in the fight for God's Glory.

Unfortunately, this entitled disease is generations of generations old, and this might be the hardest to overcome. Entitled church leaders, what is your position in the game of war?

The function of any leader is represented by the queen. The most potent piece of the entire chess game.

The king is the weakest due to his moves, only able to walk one square at a time, a complete 360, yet if he is under any attack, there is nothing he can do on his own. On the other hand, the queen can move freely throughout the battlefield. Her attacks are intense and frightening, and her only weakness is that she cannot replicate the knight's offensive as her own.

The queen is a perfect representation of any leadership position within the church. From the top of the organization to the lowest of leadership roles, her ability is best suited to the authentic characteristics that any leader must show: leading her King's army into the horrors of battle without dread of the hard work. The queen's unity in the faith is intended to be an example of expendable Glory to her King without any entitlement issues. Her passion and desire to bring victory to her King is enough to give all she has in the struggle against her enemy. If her death is required to break open a path for a revolution, she does not hesitate. Her most vital ability is to inspire the army to fight to the death. True leaders do not wait quietly for others to do what is called upon them; they take action. They show others what can be achieved if you believe in the King.

But we are not in a world filled with queens who have a true passion. Leaders nowadays have become undependable due to the illness of entitlement. This sickness brings a mentality of directorship, and only I call the shots. I am the leader; I will not follow the thoughts and inspirations of a lesser person.

Entitled is believing oneself to be inherently deserving of privileges or special treatment.

Have you seen a leader who picks up the weight of the work and stays behind to clean, walks in unity within the battle, leads with actions, and does not demand; one who shares the victory with his fellow soldiers?

If you have, stay by his side! Walk with him! If not, I say, seek to find a true leader; don't be content with those who seek entitlement as fame.

The queen's moves combine two other pieces in the game, the rook and the bishop. Both serve a particular purpose in the king's army, and if you wish to fully embrace your position as queen/leader, learn to use both bishop and rook within you.

In my first book *"Entangled"* I spoke about the helmet of God and its significance on the battlefield and how the soldiers look to the general's mark as they push against adversity. The true leaders fight side by side with their men. To be an effective leader is never to forget that you're not special; God can use a donkey. So don't be a donkey; stop acting like you're the one and only. Nothing about us is worthy of being celebrated over Christ.

I have this issue with modern-day Christianity and its superficial leaders. They surround themselves with the *wows* of men devouring garbage and praising it, leaving the rest of the population to die in battle as they hide behind the walls of their pawns' *wows* awaiting death to come knocking.

Wake up! This fantasy is coming to an end soon.

I have plenty to say about how a true queen's characteristics should represent any leader in the church. So, please keep reading because we will explore more of the need for character growth and what makes up the queen/leader in the following two chapters.

I am still learning and growing. But truth be told, those who sit and talk about how great they are, have minimal character development. If you hear someone go on and on about how great they are, just remember there is only one GREAT I AM.

CHAPTER  thirteen

Once more, I ask, just who are you?

We have already spoken to the church leaders; if you're not a leader, then who are you?

A bishop, the worshipper! The one who brings heaven to earth using song and dance. It is an honor to be a worshipper; you conduct the spectacle of faith to the congregation. We sing together towards heaven with a splendor of joy for the name of Christ. What can I say but Glory to the Almighty!

Unfittingly, the credit is often misplaced for you than for who it deserves for God.

The characteristic of a bishop displays as one of the first responders alongside the queen in battle. They move freely in an "x" pattern swift and elegances, keeping it simple for everyone; this is one part of the queen's power. As the first pawns advance, the bishop sets a visual assault on the enemy and controls potential territory within the board. Powerful when used together, the light and dark bishops stand guard beside the king and queen.

I consider them to be the worshippers of the church because they help spread the Glory of our Majesty. Their influence is imposed significantly at the beginning of the game. The bishop administers the path the pawns must take during the game, and the pawns need to open the road for the bishop to take territory for the King's army. A trapped bishop is useless and thus a worshipper who does not wisely apply his gift.

Great is the need to properly use our bishops within the church. Just like the entitled leader, the bishop has common flaws. The flaws to overstep their position, confusing what they indeed are with something else!

Take this example. A worshipper is to lead the congregation into the heavenly places, and they provide the encouragement to keep the faith; they create the atmosphere of conquerors in battle. Songs and dance are our connection to the Holy Spirit, and The commoner is touched more by the emotional song of a bishop than the written words of the King. Don't believe me? Then go to YouTube, and look at the numbers of Godly inspired sermons compared to the zealously established songs. The commoner has replaced the bishop's work as its King, yet the bishop has not corrected this error.

Do not forget the devil was once in the position of the bishop, and he had the honor to produce the inhabitants' praises and joys for the Highest deity in the Universe!

Our modern Christianity worshippers have become lost within this entitled sickness; the chants of the common person can become poison to a bishop who holds no character.

I won't go deep into the concept of the fame and disgrace we have placed upon this position; my intent is for the bishop to understand his role is more than the stage!

When a bishop/worshiper learns to lead by actions and not by the spectacle, he will be effective in battle.

Which of these do you find to have more character? Example A: the worshipper who only cares about his world, my mic, drums, and guitar. *The people must leave everything ready when I show up, or I won't play. Only I declare when and where the Holy Spirit is moving among us. I am the show; you worship to me!* Someone out there in this world truly believes this to be holy, and the sad part is people follow them!

Example B: *I am the servant; I am not unique! I will praise the Lord, and any who also serves him will join. I understand the stage is meaningless; what has true honor is giving a helping hand, and to support my brothers and sisters in trying times. This is the difference of the Holy Spirit. Not the way my songs can manipulate the ordinary man to his emotions but the true interactions with the congregation in battle.*

What type of bishop/worshiper do you see in these examples? Have you ever run across one of these? There is so much information for us to break down the proper application for the bishop. Yet, the one thing I see that can resolve many common issues within worshipers is for them to become the rook.

If they change their perspective on ministry, all sickness will fade when they learn to understand their other half. Ministry is not in the stage but the increase for exploration within the human heart.

The stage is only the introduction to an epic revolutionary event. To be victorious, our soldiers must experience faith at its most intimate; this is the job of the honest bishop to carry the banner of faith.

CHAPTER fourteen

Do you know who you are by now? Are you a bishop craving to learn what it truly means to serve? Would you say you're a queen concerned with your character's growth? Maybe you are a rook, patiently waiting your turn to help the Mighty King?

The worker is worthy of his food, says Paul. (Matthew 10:10 KJV) "...for the workman is worthy of his meat." As a result, so is the rook excellent at being the protector of his King in the end game. The two rooks are positioned to take a stronghold of both corner sections of the board. The farthest away from the King from the game's hierarchy, yet the only piece suited to guard the King's integrity from its enemy's shame.

The rook is mostly used in the later section of the game, called *the end game*, and this is when most of your significant pieces have fallen or remained inactive. The king can make an extraordinary move, but only if it is his first-ever physical move in the game; it's called castling. This is when you take your king and essentially swap places with the rook on either side of the board; the only catch is there can be no interference by your opponent or your army during this move. Castling serves to protect your king behind a deadly fortress made by the rooks and pawns; for the enemy to break through this castling defense, sacrifices must be made. Unlike the queen or bishop, the rook's power is most effective in the end game, and they don't always have the privilege to deliver a cunning victory.

The rook is designed to move in a "+" pattern, a direct and authoritative invasion toward the enemy, the final building block of the queen's power.

Due to the direct approach of the rook, they hold a special place in the King's army, the honor of carrying the authoritative dignity of the King's passion, grace, and determination of his kingdom. The workers of the church! The people who serve with loving hands, power, and care. Those who say "I" when none dare to speak, the people who do not seek the stage but seek the face of the King. The man preparing to serve, the woman decorating the wedding for the groom's arrival. The King's most loyal protector is the people who provide the services you need within the church, whether an event or just a Sunday service. The people who clean, set the stage, and prepare the food are the workers who are worthy of their food.

In an era where everyone wants to be somebody: a pastor, a worshipper, an influencer, it will leave the King to be stranded alone to perish. The common flaw in our modern-day rooks; they have forgotten that they are the protectors of our King. The sickness of entitled positions which ask for praise has spilled over into the most significant part of this war!

Every rook's function is designed to build character, to give a helping hand while the other hand stands witness to the unknown. Seek not to glorify yourself but to glorify the kingdom of God, for this is the true meaning of serving the Lord.

Do not boast about your actions, do not speak about what others do not do, but you do! If I were to say all the things I do and you do not, I have no character, so I say I don't do enough.

Rooks, learn to honor your position, do not seek recognition, for God will give you the honor in heaven. Protecting the King is serving and displaying true character within a battle.

Understand, after the pastors and worshippers have fallen, only the rooks remain! The helping hand will be the deciding factor in the End Game of the church, the time of revelation will come, and only those who support the King in the final hours with honor and determination will deliver the victorious glory for the Almighty! The testing ground for building character is found within the rook's actions.

For you to become a true rook with honor and nature of the Almighty, pursue the work of services unto your church, do not dread it but welcome it! Your food, in the end, will be worthy of your work! The question is, how flavorsome do you want it to taste?

CHAPTER  fifteen

Oh, the congregation, how mighty you are!

With only two uncovered identities remaining, which do you believe you represent! The knight or the pawns? Yes, of course, you are pawns!

The pawns are the foot soldiers of the King's army; they are weak yet strong when used wisely. They can become an impenetrable wall, a vicious barrage of attackers, or even a life source for the King's survival! The pawns are strong in numbers and useless in isolation – an outstanding representation of the potential power the congregation can hold, fighting united in one cause. This is what a group of individuals can do if they seek to work together, battle under one flag with no division and no hate within our brothers and sisters, no words of evil to spread out, and a kingdom united. That would be a remarkable accomplishment – one truly worthy of praise, a pawn loyal to his cause.

This will be the shortest chapter due to the pawns' character flaws – the flaws of abandonment to the struggle.

The congregation is mighty, but the lone soldier will always fail his King!

The pawns move only forward and can attack only towards his sides; his only objective is to follow the King's order.

The issue with the weak pawns is when they seek to become queens before becoming rooks and bishops! When a pawn reaches the final square on the edge of the board, it gains the ability to promote itself into any piece of the game except the King.

To be promoted too soon is a common problem found in our congregations. Thus, you gain the isolated pawns stranded on the battlefield awaiting the enemy's soldier to capture and humiliate them. How often do we see people promoted too soon, not having the character to support the weight of leading with honor, causing the congregation to be divided and broken?

Unable to regain the structure of unity, the King becomes exposed, and his enemy can abuse every weakness to gain the upper hand in battle.

How many examples of fallen pawns exist in the world today? Those who jump church to church never come to know true loyalty. They blame the King for their desertion in battle but never look at themselves.

Oh, the congregation, how mighty will you be when you truly learn to become united in this kingdom! If you are a pawn, do not seek to become prompted but seek to become loyal to your cause! Loyalty to the empire will bring victory, for it is much better to be a pawn for God than a queen for the enemy! "Alone we fall, together we stand."

CHAPTER  sixteen

Finally, we have reached the end, with only one remaining piece to discover.

What's that famous saying? We save the best for last! So, here we go!

The knights, better known as the horse for their unique design, provide an exclusive attribute suited best to the Holy Spirit in our church world. Its fancy moves of jumping over every piece of the game in a "360 L" pattern make the knights a vital opening for the push towards war. The same can be applied to the Holy Spirit.

I have spoken about how I believe (Acts 1:8 KJV) is the primary cause of the church's growth over time.

But since each chapter deals with the manipulation/misunderstood roles in the church, this chapter will be no different.

Sadly, the passing of time has also caused

modern Christianity to mishandle the Knights/ Holy Spirit's movements in the church.

I come from a Pentecostal background, so I can believe in the most peculiar of spiritual activities. Unfortunately, what I identify as the actual movement of God, I cannot share with you for this reason: There are millions of wild people who proclaim to be under the Spirit, yet they are not. The more time passes, the more the Spirit has become a joke within Christians. The cancerous joke crippled the church into wars and tribulation with itself. Countless videos of humiliation regarding the Holy Spirit's movement, and we as the body have done nothing to correct this!

We do not correct this simply because we don't understand the characteristics of the Spirit. The Spirit was sent as a Helper, to be a guide in the darkness of our minds. It was never meant to be controlled by our emotions or to be played as if it were a guitar, and each string is to be plucked for a tune, carefully crafted to play the most delightful songs to our hearts and soul.

God the Almighty is often represented as a quenching fire, and so is the Spirit's first introduction into the game.

Throughout time, humankind has learned to control fire through tools and engineering; from our creation, man could never psychically touch fire; thus, man gained control of that which was impossible to reach.

Nowadays, so has the Holy Spirit fallen to humanity's ways of manipulating the effects of the Spirit, causing us to have misguided Knights bring shame to our King's army.

An invincible fire has become a plaything among children of character. The lack of spiritual growth has made the Spirit's authority questioned among Christian.

Paul makes clear the importance of the Spirit in his writing. God ignites the characteristic of this fire's movement to bring conviction of oneself, leading to a revelation of repentance, establishing an atmosphere of holiness for the exploration of the uncontrolled fire, marking it the indisputable authority of the Pentecostal Spirit of God.

Yet, the church has been fooled by the *wows* of babies who crave to control this fire by crafting the fictitious model of the Spirit – kindled by man, eager for the dreams of humankind, intent on visions of success, for exploiting the sentiments of the weak, leading to the artificial fire.

Greater is the need to properly understand the Holy Spirit than the need to speak in tongues.

Church, let us correct the errors of our generation towards the Holy Spirit now before it's too late! Let us end this cancerous joke, the joke we have carelessly created by losing the knights' authority to the enemy's pawns. So, let us fight back by seeking the edification of the rushing wind pushing away man's ego for glorifying the King!

CHAPTER seventeen

Thank you for reading this far. I am no author, and I am no writer; that is why I am grateful if you have read and enjoyed this book! I would be even more thankful if you could receive a better understanding of your unique role within your church.

I will ask you to please read Paul's writing to the Corinthians to better understand the concept of this book.

My intent was not to preach to you but to enable you to fill in the blanks with your own experiences with the church world.

We all have a story of what the church world has offered to our lives, good or bad, and we cannot blame the church without blaming ourselves first. For every broken report, there is an inactive chess piece on the board, and we must learn to play our roles in order to gain the victory correctly.

The End Game is here and now. The time to fight for the kingdom's integrity has arrived! What will you do? What role will you play? The King needs loyal soldiers; his army is in a losing battle. For the church to survive, seek not man's artificial dreams but the true revelation and conviction of the Almighty.

SI VIS PACEM, PARA BELLUM. IF PEACE, PREPARE FOR WAR.

Eternal thanksgiving to all the leaders/soldiers of the Igreja Tabuas Da lei Stones of Law Church: my parents, who genuinely lead the path of a true queen in life – Pastors Josue and Waldierene Sampaio, have created a legacy to remember.

Along with people of true character who have followed behind, jumping into the fray: pastors Gilmar and Rosileia Rodrigues, pastor Ana Flávia and her husband preb. Danilo Oliveira, evangelists Armand and Janaina Scipione, pastors Nilton and Simone de Souza. And to the whole body of this house's deacons, deaconesses, and workers. Especially being the longest deaconess, Teresa Sabino.

They are faithful leaders to the body of Christ Jesus.

ABOUT THE AUTHOR

Elias C Sampaio is a young pastor in "Igreja Tabuas Da lei Stones of Law Church," Boca Raton, Florida. Christ for the Nations Institute graduate 2020, Pastoral Major.

Printed in the United States
by Baker & Taylor Publisher Services